T0198802

AuthorHouse™
1663 Liberty Drive
Bloomington, IN 47403
www.authorhouse.com
Phone: 1 (800) 839-8640

Published by AuthorHouse 09/02/2016

ISBN: 978-1-5246-3803-0 (sc)
978-1-5246-3804-7 (e)

Library of Congress Control Number: Pending

Print information available on the last page.

authorHOUSE®

WRINGLES & SNIGGLES

DISCOVER AMERICA

George Evans

Chapter One

Somewhere in the Midwest, there lived a worm called Wringles. He was a happy and a curious worm. He wiggled and wiggled from the day he was born. His family giggled whenever Wringles wiggled. Sometimes he accidentally wiggled into trouble; but he usually found a way to wiggle out of it. During the family outings he often lagged far behind and got lost. So his mother knitted a bright red cap so he could be easily found. Wringles liked his cap so much he never took it off. He even wore it to bed. But he had to remove it during dinner.

It had rained hard all day and the ground was too wet, even for worms. Streams of fast- moving water filled the street gutters.

Before finishing dinner, the father said, "We have to leave now!" The entrance was blocked with mud. So, the father quickly made an escape tunnel and everyone followed, except Wringle who was looking for his hat he had misplaced during all of the commotion. Meanwhile, the family had safely crawled up onto a large rock under a tree; but where was Wringles?

The worried father rushed back to their home as fast as he could. He called out, "Wringles" several times.

But there was no answer.

The father returned with the sad news. The family planned to look for him after the rain had stopped.

Wringles was stuck in the mud. He struggled and struggled until he finally broke free. He was about to crawl out when the ground shook. The footsteps became louder and louder.

Then, suddenly, a shovel dug deep into the ground. Wringles tried to escape; but it was too late.

The fisherman looked at the shovel of dirt and said, "Well, we found at least one worm, but he's not very big. Son, put it in the can. Let's go dig over there."

Wringles was one of many worms trapped in a can. He introduced himself. "Hi, my name is Wringles."

1.

A wise, old worm looked at Wringles and said, "Well, I see they caught you too. I wouldn't worry too much since the fishermen prefer bigger and fatter worms at the end of a fish hook. Why are you wearing a red hat?

"If I get lost, my parents could find me. What's a fish hook?"

"Well, people use worms for bait to catch fish."

"What happens then?"

"Well, it won't be good. The fish like to eat worms." .

"I don't want to be fish bait. We have to get out of here."

"We tried; but the can is too tall and slippery."

Wringles thought for a moment and said, "I know what we can do.

Let's all wiggle together as hard as we can."

All of the worms wiggled and wiggled until the can jiggled. The can jiggled and jiggled and sure enough the can toppled over. They all cheered and crawled out as fast as they could. They were now free to go home.

Wringles felt quite good that his idea worked and he wiggled with pride and joy. The sun became hotter and hotter. Wringles took cover under a leaf, remembering how his mother had taught him to keep out of the hot sun. He came out at sunset and Wringles searched for his family late into the night. Poor Wringles was all alone. He cried himself to sleep.

Strange noises awakened him up early in the morning before sunrise. Curious, he dug a tunnel to take a look. A black bird with yellow wings was pecking at the ground, hunting for his breakfast. Wringles quickly returned to his hiding place and remained as quiet as he could be until the bird flew away.

Wringles looked everywhere for his family. He looked under leaves. He looked under rocks and asked other worms about his family. Wringles was very sad and he no longer felt like wiggling.

Wringles decided to rest and crawled inside a pile of leaves. Everything was fine until a sudden gust of wind blew the leaves and Wringles into a fast-moving sream. He quickly climbed on to a small branch and before he knew it, he was floating in a large lake. Wringles became very afraid. How much longer could he hold onto the branch?

2.

The wind and the waves rocked the branch up and down. He held on with all of his strength. When Wringles thought all hope was lost, he saw a small boat with an old man, half asleep, holding a fishing pole. Fortunately, the waves pushed the branch and Wringles next to the boat. Wringles had to make a difficult decision. If he stayed on the branch, he could either drown or be cooked by the sun. Or, he could take a chance by getting into the boat and becoming fish bait. Wringles climbed up the oar and then he jumped to the bottom of the boat. Fortunately, the fisherman didn't see him. Wringles was very tired and he soon fell fast asleep in a dark corner.

The morning light woke up Wringles. The fisherman was gone and the boat was tied to a post. Wringles went up the sides of the boat and then he jumped onto the pier. As you know, little worms can't travel very fast and Wringles had a long ways to go. When he became tired he stopped to rest under the shade of a tree until the clouds hid the hot sun. Then he continued his journey home. Just before nightfall Wringles finally reached his old neighborhood.

Excited to be home again, he quickly crawled through the entrance and Wringles surprised everyone. They all wiggled and giggled with joy.

The father said, "Son, we're all very happy to see you safe at home. We were very worried."

3.

Wringles Meets a Mouse and an Eagle

Chapter Two

Wringles was up earlier than usual and he decided to explore a different neighborhood. After he finished his breakfast, Wringles was on his way out the door when his mother asked,

"Where are you going so early in the morning?"

"I just want to get out of the house and play with a few friends."

"Be careful of the birds and stay out of the sun. Don't forget your cap."

"I know, Mom and don't worry. I'll be back in time for lunch."

While Wringles was enjoying the crisp, cool morning air, hoping to find someone to play with he heard a call for help.

He followed the squeaky voice that led him to a neighbor's backyard. Wringles crawled through a small opening in the fence. The call for help became louder and louder. Finally, Wringles saw a mouse struggling to free its tail caught in a trap. The small mouse was exhausted and he was about to give up hope. Then he saw Wringles.

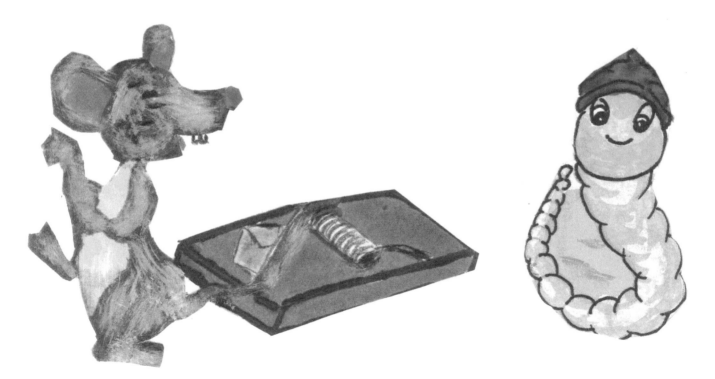

The mouse pleaded, "Please help me."

Wringles searched for something to help the poor mouse.

Then the mouse sneezed not once but twice. Worried, the mouse said, "Please hurry, the neighbor's cat is getting closer."

"How do you know?"

"I'm allergic to cats."

Wringles found a small stick and he lifted the spring just enough for the mouse to pull his tail free from the mouse trap. The mouse now looked a little different with his crooked tail.

Before the mouse could thank Wringles, he sneezed louder than ever. "Ah, Ah, Ah Choo!" 4.

The mouse said, " Hurry, climb on my back. We have to leave now!

"First, tell me your name. I'm Wringles."

"I'll tell you later. Hold on tight."

The mouse ran as fast as he could to his favorite hiding place, a small hole in the wall. They barely escaped the cat's long, sharp claws. Whenever the mouse was about to sneeze, Wringles covered his mouth with his red cap. They were as quiet as a "church mouse." Tired of waiting, the frustrated cat finally left. When they felt that it was safe they came out of their hiding place.

"Now I can tell you my name. My mother named me Sniggles."

Sniggles thanked Wringles for saving his life. It was the beginning of a close friendship. Wringles could now go further and faster on the back of a new friend with a crooked tail.

Sniggles scurried about. Wringles had to hold onto his cap as Sniggles jumped up and down like a bouncing ball. They never had so much fun.

Sniggles ran up a large hill. As soon as they reached the top, Sniggles said, "Let's slide down this hill on a leaf." Wringles liked the idea. They found a large, shiny leaf and as soon as they were ready, Sniggles pushed off with his foot and said, "Hold on tight. Here we go."

Down the hill they went. Sniggles ears were pushed back by the wind as they raced down the bumpy hill. They laughed at the thrill of going faster and faster, nearly running into trees. They zigged and zagged all the way down, unaware of the danger ahead of them.

Suddenly, the hill came to an abrupt end. They were going too fast to stop and before they knew it they were flying off a high cliff holding onto the leaf. Wringles and Sniggles stopped laughing and became scared as they fell through the air. The two helpless victims were falling faster and faster. It looked hopeless.

Just as they were about to plunge into the fast-moving river a large claw snatched them from certain death. Then the eagle flapped his powerful wings and up he flew to a large nest at the top of the tallest tree. Wringles and Sniggles shivered with fear as the eagle stared at them without saying a word. It looked like it was the end of Wringles and Sniggles.

Wringles gathered all of his courage, looked at the eagle and said, "I don't think you'll like eating us. We don't taste very good,"

5.

Sniggles joined in, "Yea. We taste terrible and we'll give you a stomach ache."

The eagle blinked his big, blue eyes and laughed, "You're not even one small bite. You're lucky that I'm different from other eagles. I only eat fish. I wouldn't waste my time eating a mouse and a little worm with a funny red cap."

Insulted, Sniggles complained, "So, we're not good enough for you."

Wringles placed his cap over Sniggles' mouth before he could say another word and apologized.

The eagle smiled, "There's nothing to worry about. I just wanted to do my good deed for the day. If you want a real ride, hop on. By the way, my name is Kohana. It's an Indian name that means swift and brave."

Greatly relieved, Wringles and Sniggles felt safe on the broad, strong back of an American Bald Eagle. In an instant, the three were flying above fluffy, white clouds. Kohana soared with grace as his seven-foot wing span glided with the winds, leaning to the left and then to the right, making great circles in the sky. It was much more fun and exciting than sliding down a hill on a leaf.

Kohana turned his head and asked, "Where would you two like to go?"

Wringles answered, "I've never seen snow."

Sniggles asked, "Could we first go to the city where my cousins live?"

Kohana changed directions and headed for the city. While they were on their way an angry eagle didn't like the idea of strangers entering his territory. Sniggles saw him coming from behind and warned Kohana. Kohana wasn't one to fly away from a fight; but he had his friends to worry about. So Kohana flew as fast as he could. Wringles and Sniggles became afraid and held on tightly. The eagle rammed into Kohana, knocking Sniggles and Wringles off Kohana's back. They were falling fast and screaming. Kohana went after his two friends and grabbed them with his claws. Then he gently put them down on the ground.

Kohana said, "Wait here. I'll be back in a minute."

Kohana flew straight up. His friendly eyes took on a fierce look. The two great eagles clashed head on. The high-pitched shrieks could be heard for miles around. Wringles and Sniggles watched the fight and hoped that Kohana would not get hurt. It was long before the defeated eagle flew back to his nest to lick his wounds. Kohana, losing only a few feathers, returned to his two friends and they continued their peaceful flight to the city.

6.

Wringles and Sniggles were both amazed to see such tall the buildings and the traffic jams. The sounds of the honking horns hurt their ears. From above, people looked like confused ants running in all directions. Sniggles couldn't stop sneezing and Wringles eyes were burning from the dirty air.

Sniggles could hardly breathe. "I've seen enough. Let's get out of here. I really feel sorry for my cousins."

Kohana changed directions. He headed for the mountains and clean air.

From hundreds of feet up, Wringles and Sniggles could see for miles. Kohana flew over forests and clear, blue lakes. It was getting too cold for Wringles; so he crawled under Kohana's soft feathers to keep warm.

As they approached the snow-capped mountains, Sniggles told Wringles to take a look. Wringles came out from his warm spot and marveled at the beauty of the snow glittering in the sun as Kohana circled the mountains. They saw wolves, bears, and elk roaming freely in the lush green valley.

After the brief tour, Kohana dropped off his passengers and soared up to look for fish. With his keen eyesight, he spotted a large fish in the stream. He folded his wings back and dived. He grabbed the fish with his claws and then flew to a quiet spot near the river bank to eat his lunch. While Kohana was busy eating, Wringles and Sniggles decided to explore the area.

Suddenly, Sniggles sneezed twice. They both knew what that meant and yelled for help. Kohana heard them and he quickly took off in flight. From above Kohana saw a mountain lion that was about to pounce on his friends. Kohana swooped down and bit the unsuspecting mountain lion with his sharp beak. The mountain lion turned and tried to snatch Kohana out of the air with his claws. But Kohana was too quick. Then, Kohana attacked the lion again. The mountain lion was quick to realize that he had to look for his food elsewhere. He turned and ran into the woods.

In their haste, Wringles lost his red cap. They climbed on Kohana's back and he circled low until they found it. Wringles brushed off his cap and thanked Kohana and asked, "What time is it?"

Kohana looked at the sun and said, "It's about three."

Worried, Wringles said, "I've already missed lunch and I better not be late for dinner. My parents will really be worried."

"Hurry, climb on." Kohana flew as fast as he could..

7.

Kohana glided down for a landing in the neighborhood where his friends lived. They thanked Kohana for the exciting ride and hoped to see him again.

Kohana looked at his two small friends and said, "Try to stay out of trouble."

"We promise."

Kohana smiled and then he swooped up and he was soon out of sight.

Wringles quickly climbed onto Sniggle's back and off they went.

Before they went their separate ways, Wringles commented, " Kohana is a good friend. He really cares about us."

"Yea. We're very lucky. Let's meet tomorrow and go see Kohana."

As Wringles entered the kitchen his mother asked, "What did you do all day?"

"Not much, just another boring day. Sorry I missed lunch."

"You always give me the same answer when I ask about school. You must have done something all day."

"Well, mom, if you must know. I saved a mouse from a big cat. We rode on a leaf down a hill and we fell off a cliff. We were lucky a big eagle saved us. The eagle took us to to the city and an eagle attacked us. The sudden jolt knocked us off Kohana's back and he saved us again. Our courageous friend flew at him and they fought. Kohana won the fight.

He then took us to the city. After that, we saw the snow-capped mountains. The eagle was hungry and he dropped us off while he searched the river for a fish. A mountain lion was about to eat my new friend, Sniggles. We yelled for help and Kohana chased the lion away. It was getting late so the eagle brought us back home."

Mother smiled, "Son, you have such a vivid imagination. You ought to write children's stories. Take off your hat. It's time for dinner."

8.

The Birth of America

Chapter Three

While Wringles was eating breakfast, his father reminded him about the Fourth of July parade and asked, "Do you know why we celebrate the Fourth of July?"

"Sure, I know. There's a lot of fireworks and parades."

Father smiled, "That's only partly true. Someday you'll learn why we celebrate the Fourth of July."

After breakfast, Wringles put on his red hat and went over to Sniggles' home and found him fast asleep. He tried to wake him up; but he didn't blink an eye. Finally, Wringles made a sound like a cat. Sniggles jumped out of bed and hid in the closet.

Laughing, "It's okay. It's just me, Wringles."

Sniggles came out of hiding and Wringles told him about the parade. Wringles climbed on Sniggles' back and off they went. People were lined up three deep and applauded as the bands and colorful floats passed by. Sniggles and Wringles stretched their necks but they couldn't see much from the sewer drain.

Wringles said, "This is really fun and exciting."

"If you want to see excitement, watch this," commented Sniggles.

Sniggles jumped out in front of the majorettes. They dropped their batons and screamed as they ran.

People shouted, "Get that mouse!" The well-planned parade was suddenly replaced with chaos and confusion. The bands stopped playing. In fact, the parade came to a complete standstill as people rushed about trying to catch a little, harmless mouse. But Sniggles was too elusive and he safely returned to the sewer drain.

"Wow, you really did stir up a lot of excitement," said Wringles.

"It always happens. For some reason people get all excited and become afraid whenever they see me."

After that incident, Sniggles took Wringles over to a nearby building where Sniggles climbed up a few steps. Then he scurried over to a large window overlooking the parade for a clear view. By now the parade was back to normal. In front of one of the floats, boy and girl scouts proudly carried flags. On one of the flags was a picture of a bald eagle with wide spread wings, a blue shield on its chest, 13 red and white stripes and 13

9.

stars. In his right talon, he held an olive branch and in his left talon he had a bundle of 13 arrows. His beak held a scroll with an inscription, "E Pluribus Unum." Wringles and Sniggles were further impressed when they saw a shiny brass eagle at the top of each flag pole. They both wondered why their friend, Kohana, was so popular. Also, they didn't understand the meaning of "E Pluribus Unum" and what was so important about the number thirteen?

After the parade, they went to see their friend, Kohana. Standing next to his tree, they called out his name again and again. But there was no answer. They gave up and decided to go play in the nearby fields. While playing, they didn't notice a rattlesnake slowly sneaking up on Sniggles, who was having so much fun playing hide and seek. The snake quietly slithered closer and closer. Sniggles happened to turn around and noticed something moving under a pile of leaves. Frightened, he ran as fast as he could; but the snake was gaining on him. Just as the snake was about to bite Sniggles, Kohana's large claws grabbed the snake, carried it across the river and released it.

Kohana returned to his friends and said, "We always seem to meet when you two are in trouble."

Wringles said, "At the parade we saw a flag with a picture of you holding 13 arrows and a branch. Also, there was a brass eagle on top of the flag pole. Why are you so famous and why do we celebrate the Fourth of July?"

Kohana smiled and said, "The thirteen arrows and thirteen stars stand for the original thirteen colonies now called states. The colonies were once owned by a country, called England or Great Britain that's thousands of miles from here. "E Pluribus Unum" means: out of many, one."

Wringles asked, "What does that mean?"

"It means that even though our country is made up of people from all over the world with different skin colors and beliefs, we are all Americans and we should work together as one country in order to prosper and always ready to protect our freedom."

"Sniggles also wondered, "Does that include us?"

"I guess you could say that. The important thing to remember is we're very fortunate to live in America."

Sniggles agreed, "I'm grateful to live here."

"Me too," said Wringles.

Kohana, "Yes, we should all be grateful. Sometimes we forget that we live in a great country. Meet me here early tomorrow morning and I'll show you why we celebrate the fourth of July and how our great country grew." 10.

Wringles and Sniggles met Kohana the following morning and they climbed onto Kohana's back. Kohana quickly soared high above the tree tops with his powerful wings and headed east. Wringles and Sniggles had no idea where their friend was taking them.

Sniggles kept asking every five minutes, "Are we there yet?"

After a long flight, they finally arrived in Philadelphia, Pennsylvania. Kohana landed on a large branch overlooking a huge bronze bell with a crack from top to bottom.

Wringles said, "Wow! That's a big bell. How much does it weigh?"

Kohana answered, "It weighs 2080 pounds and it's about four feet across."

Sniggles asked, "What was it used for?"

Kohana answered, "First, I'll tell you a little history about it. The bell was made in England in 1753. It was placed in the steeple of the Pennsylvania State House and somebody rang the bell when it was time for a meeting or a town emergency. After more than 100 years, the bell was named the "Liberty Bell" because it rang to celebrate the reading of the Declaration of Independence in Philadelphia on July 8, 1776. It's uncertain when and why the bell cracked. The "Liberty Bell" rang for all of the people's freedom."

Sniggles then asked, "What does the Declaration of Independence mean?"

Kohana answered, "It was a letter to King George III of England written by Thomas Jefferson. John Adams and Benjamin Franklin also helped write it. Fifty-six brave men, who represented the people living in the colonies, proudly signed the letter into law on July 4, 1776. The king became very angry and wanted to punish those who signed it."

"What was the letter to the king about?" asked Wringles.

"The main idea of the letter could be summed up with one sentence. 'All men are created equal and have the right to life, liberty and the pursuit of happiness.' In other words, the people wanted to make their own laws, free to make their own choices and not be told what to do by a king thousands of miles away. The colonists wanted to form their own democratic government."

Both Wringles and Sniggles asked, "What's that?"

Kohana smiled and said, "You certainly ask the right questions. A democratic government means that Americans can vote for someone to speak for them at meetings where laws are passed. If their representative doesn't do what the majority of the voters want, then the people will vote for someone else. So, it's very important to vote." 11.

"Were there any other reasons why the colonists wanted to form their own government?" asked Sniggles.

"Yes, there were. The king was a cruel and an unjust king. Since he needed more money to pay for the war against the French, he increased the already high taxes. Also, he didn't respect the people's rights and property. Then, an unusual and daring thing happened in Boston. A few of the colonists, dressed as Indians, dumped several boxes of English tea in the water, protesting the heavy tax on tea. It was called the "Boston Tea Party."

"What did the king do?" asked Wringles.

"Well, the king had already sent soldiers in 1775 to stop the 13 colonies from each trying to form their own government and appointed General Gage as the governor to defeat the rebels; but many of the rebels, called minutemen, were determined to be free and they were not afraid of the king's large, trained army and navy. So, the Revolutionary War began. The chances of winning the war were slim but the brave colonists desperately wanted to be free and they were fortunate that France, Spain and Holland secretly gave the rebels weapons, ammunition and supplies. Besides not getting along with England, France was afraid that England would be a threat to their large land holdings west of the Mississippi.

"Who were the minutemen and where was the first battle?" wondered Sniggles, while scratching his head.

"Minutemen were always ready to fight the British at a minute's notice. In many homes, a rifle was within easy reach, usually mounted above the front door. Then, it took thirty seconds for a person to reload for only one shot..The first battles were in the towns of Lexington and Concord. The Continental Congress was made of up a group of men who represented the colonies and they chose George Washington to be the commander of the first continental army. It wasn't much of an army. There was little or no money to pay the soldiers who weren't very well trained and the soldiers lived in harsh conditions. An army officer from another country, who believed in their cause, trained our men how to fight as soldiers."

"I guess we were lucky to have help from other countries," said Wringles.

"Yes, we were very fortunate; but thousands of lives were lost on both sides and there was a great deal of destruction. War is a terrible waste and disagreements should be settled peacefully; but sometimes it's not possible."

Sniggles asked, "What were some of the other battles?"

Kohana had to stop and think awhile and then said, "There were many battles and we lost a few of them. But before I tell you about a couple of battles, it's important to mention that General George Washington did a daring thing to boost the morale of the tired, hungry and cold soldiers. Also, the people at home were worried that the war wasn't going well and many of them thought it was a mistake to go against the king's mighty army."

Wringles asked, "What did General Washington do?"

"Well, on December 25th, 1776, Christmas morning, Washington's army crossed the Delaware River during a severe snow blizzard. Large chunks of ice were pushed aside by men in the boat to allow the boats to go through. The unexpected invasion surprised the sleeping enemy at fort Trenton, New Jersey. Our army lost only a few men. The success of this bold move led to other victories and inspired more men to join the army. Also, the people at home were encouraged and donated more money to the war effort."

Wringles asked, "But where do you come in?"

Kohana smiled and said, "No one knows for sure. One story is that during a battle one morning, the noise woke up the eagles in a nearby nest and the angry eagles circled above the soldiers and gave out cries of complaints. One of the soldiers yelled, "They are shrieking for freedom." Or another story is Americans thought that the eagle only existed in North America. Then, Kohana puffed up his chest, stood a little taller, head up high and with a proud voice said, "Probably the best answer to your question as to why I was chosen to be the American symbol is people thought I was noble, smart, courageous, strong and beautiful."

Sniggles furrowed his brow and said, "I prefer the first story. Could we now hear about the war?"

"We didn't have a navy then and the French navy came to our rescue when it defeated the British navy at Chesapeake Bay, allowing us to win the battle of Yorktown in 1781. In 1783, an agreement of surrender was signed by the General Cornwallis and George Washington. Congress approved it in January, 1784 and the king signed the document in April of 1784. The documents were then exchanged in Paris on May, 1784 and the war was officially over. It was called the "Treaty of Paris."

Sniggles asked, "Why did it take so long to sign all of those documents?"

Wingles eyes lit up and said, "I know why. In those days there were no cars, trains, phones, airplanes or computers and every letter was carried by horseback, wagons or by ships."

Sniggles wondered, "Then what happened?"

Kohana said, "After the war ended, we became a nation as far north as Canada, west to the Mississippi River and south to Florida."

13.

Wringles asked, "Isn't our country bigger than that?"

After a short pause, Kohana continued, "I'll explain it later. We were finally free and at peace; but we didn't have a central government to run the country until men, who were elected by the people of each colony, met and formed a congress to pass laws. It was called the Continental Congress. But it had little or no power. There was no money, nor was there a president or a judicial system. In order to prevent anyone or any group from becoming too powerful, three branches of government were formed as a check and balance system at the constitutional convention in Philadelphia in 1787. James Madison wrote the first draft of the Constitution and members of congress made a few changes."

"What are the three branches?" asked Sniggles.

"The executive branch is the president of the United States. Congress is the legislative branch and it's made up of representatives from the states.The third branch is the judicial branch or the Supreme Court. It's the highest court in the country that consists of nine judges appointed for life by the president and approved by the legislative branch. Congress debates and writes the laws and the president can introduce a law. Also, the president can either approve or reject a law passed by congress and if a law were in question, the Supreme Court would decide whether or not the law was just and constitutional."

"Wow, that sounds complicated." exclaimed Wringles.

"It can become complicated and change is slow; but it is far better to have the people in charge of the central government instead of having an unjust king."

Wringles smiled with confidence and proudly said, "Yea, our democracy has worked for more than 240 years."

Kohana said, "You're right and democracy would work even better if more people voted. We were so excited about our democracy that we wanted to spread it to the unsettled parts of our country and that wasn't easy. Now, I'll tell you how we became a bigger country."

Wringles commented, "This is really interesting."

Kohana continued, "The foundation of our central government was in place but the states were going in different directions and weren't working together as one country. Finally, a few states west of the Mississippi River voluntarily turned over their lands to the central government and helped set up a system to admit other states to the country. But several states still refused to accept the Constitution until a Bill of Rights or Amendments to the Constitution became an important part of it. So James Madison wrote the first Bill of Rights and a few changes were made by the legislature."

14.

Wringles asked, "What's the Bill of Rights?"

"It's a list of rules that guarantee and protect people's rights and liberties. The men who wrote it wanted to limit the powers of the government. Even with the Bill of Rights, it took a great deal of discussion before all of the states approved the constitution. New York became the location of the first national capital. George Washington and John Adams were sworn in as the first president and vice president in April, 1789, at the Federal Hall in lower Manhattan, New York."

Sniggles wondered, "What did people do for a living?"

"Good question! Since we had acres of rich soil and good climate, farmers grew and sold corn, wheat, rice, tobacco, vegetables and cotton. Also, flour, pork, bacon, lard, feathers, cider, butter and cheese were sold and shipped out of the New Orleans port located in the state of Louisiana. Skilled craftsmen made and sold things to Americans as well as to other countries. We, in turn, bought things made in other countries. Taxes on the sale of these products gave the government enough money to afford an army and a navy.

"When are you going to tell us how our country got bigger?" asked Wringles

"I'm coming to that. President Thomas Jefferson knew that Napoleon, the emperor of France, needed money to pay for his army and navy. After Napoleon conquered Spain, France acquired Spain's possessions in our country; which included a large section of land west of the Mississippi to the Rocky Mountains. Also,

President Jefferson wanted to ensure that Americans could safely use the Mississippi River to transport and trade their products. In addition, it was important to have free access to the sea port in New Orleans. So, the president decided to buy 828,800 square miles of land from France that was located in the center of our country."

"How much did the land cost and where did the president get all that money?" asked Wringles.

"We had some extra money from trading and taxes. The president offered three million dollars in gold and the government sold 12 million dollars worth of bonds. President Jefferson was surprised that Napoleon accepted the 15 million dollars in 1803. It was called the Louisiana Purchase."

Sniggles asked, "What are bonds?"

"When the government needs money, it borrows from the people by selling bonds; which is a written promise to pay it back with interest. For example, if you bought a five-year bond from the government for $100, the government would pay you the hundred dollars plus a little extra money in five years."

Wringles said, "I guess people have to trust the government to pay the money back."

15.

Sniggles said, "Fifteen million dollars was a lot of money then."

"Yes it was and many representatives didn't like the idea and they voted against buying the land. The president did what he could to change their minds. After many days of discussion, congress finally agreed to buy the land and it passed by only two votes."

"So what happened to the land we bought?" inquired Wringles.

"The land was divided into states and state boundaries were established."

"How were the state boundaries decided?"

"Rivers, access to ports and mountain ranges were normally used to set boundaries. Also, religious differences among the early settlers played a major role in determining state boundaries.

Sniggles asked, "What happened to the Indians? My father told me they were the first people here."

"We fought the Indians for more land and won since we had better weapons and more men. Many Indian tribes were forced to move to reservations and their way of life was changed forever. Also, we didn't honor all of our agreements with the Indians and we didn't treat them very well. Now it's time to meet a special lady. Climb aboard."

It wasn't long before Kohana landed on top of a large torch held up by the Statue of Liberty located on Bedloe's Island in the New York Harbor.

"Wow!" She's big!" said Wringles..

"Yes, she is. She's 151 feet tall. She represents Libertas, the Roman Goddess of Freedom, designed and made by Frederic Bartholdi. It was a gift from France to commemorate our independence and dedicated on October 28, 1806. The tablet she's holding has the inscription, July 4, 1776."

Kohana took his passengers down to the pedestal and read aloud the words carved in stone by Emma Lazarus, "Give me your tired, your poor, your huddled masses yearning to breathe free."

Kohana continued, "You should know that 80 percent of the money to build the pedestal for the statue was donated by poor immigrants who were grateful to live in America."

"Why was the statue placed here?" asked Sniggles.

"So that the thousands of people from other countries who came by boat would know that when they saw the Statue of Liberty they knew they were finally in America after a long, difficult voyage," explained Kohana. 16.

Looking up, Kohana said, "Looks like a storm is coming this way. We had better leave."

 Kohana swooped up high and then leveled off for a long flight home. Tired, Wiggles and Sniffles snuggled under Kohana's warm feathers and dozed off. Meanwhile, Kohana flew as fast as he could; but the strong cross winds made it extremely difficult for him to fly. He soon became very tired and looked for a safe place to rest until the storm blew over. But all he could see for miles were vast fields of wheat and corn. The storm became more intense and the strong gusts of wind battered Kohana about and he struggled to stay on course. The booming sounds of thunder woke up Sniggles and Wringles. They looked out from under the feathers and became afraid when they saw lightning bolts flash across the storm clouds. They held on tight as the strong winds tried to shake them loose. Kohana became worried about his friends and luckily, he saw an old cabin at the edge of a forest. He glided down to a safe landing and they rushed inside.

Kohana shook his wet feathers dry while Sniggles and Wringles searched the deserted cabin for food. All they found was one can of beans. But how were they going to open it?

Kohana said, "Step aside."

He punched holes with his sharp, powerful beak while his friends watched in amazement.. Beans had never tasted so good.

Kohana said, "While we're waiting for the storm to pass over I'll tell you about the war between the southern and northern states."

"I thought that the Constitution and the Bill of Rights solved all of the differences among the states." stated Wringles.

Kohana replied, "Not quite. Remember the Declaration of Independence stated that All Men Are Created Equal and Have the Right to Life, Liberty and the Pursuit of Happiness. Well, there was a group of people who were not treated as free men."

Puzzled, Sniggles asked, "Which group are you talking about?" It doesn't sound fair."

"People with dark skin, mostly from Africa, were brought here against their will and sold as slaves to owners of cotton and tobacco plantations. Unfortunately, a few of the slaves were treated badly by their owners. Since slavery was highly profitable, several countries bought and sold slaves long before we did. Because slaves were considered to be property, they didn't enjoy the same freedoms and the privileges as white people. President Lincoln wanted to phase out slavery; but the southern states didn't like that idea. Consequently, eleven southern states broke away from the United States and formed the Confederate States. Jefferson Davis was chosen as their president.

The Union army had a bigger army since there were twenty states in the North that had already abolished slavery." 17.

"Sounds like the South didn't have a chance. Why did they want to fight the North?" asked Wringles.

"Because cotton was the South's main industry. Also, they wanted to preserve their proud, traditional way of life without any interference from the North."

Sniggles asked, "When did the Civil War start?"

"It began on April 12, 1861, when the confederate army attacked a military base at Ft. Sumpter in South Carolina. President Lincoln immediately ordered a blockade on the Mississippi River to stop the South from shipping cotton to help pay for the war. In spite of the blockade, Robert E. Lee, a highly-respected southern general, led his army to victories in Virginia. Even though slavery was legally abolished when President Lincoln signed the Emancipation Proclamation in 1862 the war continued. The war was not going well for the North until General George Gordon Mead's army defeated General Lee at Gettysburg, Pennsylvania. It was the bloodiest battle of the war where more than 55,000 men on both sides were killed and wounded from July 1 to July 3, 1863. President Lincoln made his most memorable speech at Gettysburg on November 19, 1863, honoring the courageous soldiers on both sides.

"That was a lot of men." sadly said Wringles

"Yes, it was America's greatest tragedy. Fortunately, it was the turning point of the war. Since most of the fighting had taken place in the South, many homes were burned to the ground and properties were destroyed, creating hate and bitterness in the South for generations. After General Sherman of the Union army captured Atlanta, Georgia, General Lee surrendered to General Grant at the Appomattox Court House in Virginia on April 9, 1865. More that 600,000 men lost their lives during the Civil War."

Kohan continued. "Even though President Lincoln did his best to alleviate the South's resentment and anger, three men from the South planned to kill the president, the vice president and the Secretary of State, hoping that the government would then collapse. The vice president and Secretary of State survived the plot; but President Lincoln was shot in the head on Good Friday, April 14, 1865."

"Who killed Lincoln?" asked Wringles.

"John Wilkes Booth, an actor from the South who wanted to become a hero, shot the president while he and his wife, Mary Todd, were watching the play "Our American Cousin" at the Ford Theatre in Washington, D.C. The vast majority of the southerners did not approve of Booth's horrific act and he became an outcast."

Sniggles asked, "Did they catch him?" 18.

"Yes. He was hunted down and shot while hiding in a barn. President Lincoln is considered to be one of our greatest presidents. In a sense, he gave his life over the issue of slavery in order to keep our country together."

Sniggles asked, "Do the dark-skinned and white people get along now?"

"Better than in the past; but for years there have been many disagreements and conflicts regarding the constitutional rights of African Americans. It was a shameful period in our history. Finally, several years later, the Civil Rights Law, enforced by the federal government and soldiers, gave African Americans their constitutional rights. Change in people's attitudes is often very slow and sometimes painful. Even today there's unfair treatment of dark-skinned people. Some people have a difficult time accepting and respecting people who are different. There's an old expression: Birds of a feather gather together."

By now, the storm had passed over. Kohana turned to his friends and in a stern voice said, "Both of you stay put and don't get into any trouble while I go fishing."

"Don't worry. We won't," promised Wringles.

It didn't take very long before Sniggles became restless and wanted to explore the area. Wringles tried to talk him out of it; but Sniggles was determined to go outside. There was no stopping him and so Wringles climbed on Sniggles back and off they went. Meanwhile, Kohana had caught a large fish in a nearby river

The storm's strong winds had broken many tree branches and made it difficult for Sniggles to run; but he managed to climb and jump over them. The cool, clean air was refreshing as Sniggles happily scampered through the forest. After awhile, Wringles decided to jump off and play. Unfortunately, a branch, damaged by the strong winds, broke loose and fell on Wringles. He was pinned down and yelled for help.

Sniggles came running and he tried with all of his strength to lift the branch; but it was too heavy. He had to find Kohana fast. Sniggles ran through the forest yelling for help. Kohana heard him and he didn't like the idea of leaving his half-eaten fish behind. Kohana saw Sniggles from the air and swooped down.

"Now what is it?" asked an irritated eagle.

"Well, ahh, Wringles is trapped under a big branch."

Sniggles showed Kohana where Wringles was and Kohana easily lifted the branch with his beak. Squiggles had a few bruises; but he was okay.

Kohana didn't have to say a word. His angry stare was enough.

19.

Sniggles had to change the subject fast. He said, "In school we're learning the words to our National Anthem."

Kohana's frown changed to a smile and said, "I'm glad that you brought that up. During the War of 1812 with Great Britain, the British fired cannons all night at Fort McHenry located in Chesapeake Bay. When the smoke cleared at dawn, Francis Scott Key was inspired to write a poem when he saw a tattered American flag still waving at the top of the flag pole after the British had retreated. His poem was originally titled "Defense of Fort McHenry." Later, Thomas Carr, owner of a music store in Baltimore, gave it its present title, "The Star Spangled Banner" and it was eventually set to the tune of a popular British song, "Anacreon in Heaven." President Woodrow Wilson signed an executive order designating the poem to be our National Anthem in 1916 and congress finally declared it to be our National Anthem in 1931. The original flag was quite large. It measured 30 by 42 feet. It had only 15 stars, representing 15 states and as more states became part of the country, more stars were added. However, because a storm was heading their way, a "storm flag," measuring 17 by 25 feet, was raised and it became the battered flag that inspired Francis Scott Key to write a poem that became our National Anthem."

Sniggles said, "I'd like to learn the words to the national anthem?"

Kohana said, "Since you're interested I'll recite the words to only the first verse since it's what is always sung at special events. There are really four versus. Listen carefully."

"Oh, say can you see by the dawn's early light

What so proudly we hailed at the twilights last gleaming?

Who's broad stripes and bright stars through the perilous fight.

O'er the ramparts we watched were so gallantly streaming?

And the rockets red glare! The bombs bursting in air!

Gave proof through the night that our flag was still there.

Oh, say does that star-spangled banner yet wave

O'er the land of the free and the home of the brave?"

Wringles and Sniggles smiled with approval and promised to learn the words.

After a long flight, it was a welcome sight to see their homes again. Before they went their separate ways, Kohana said, "Meet me in the morning and we'll visit another historical place."

After they thanked Kohana, Sniggles rushed Wringles back to his home.

As expected, Wringles was late for dinner and his parents asked where he was all day and why his red cap was so dirty and damp.

Wringles had a ready answer. " I guess I like to play in the cool, wet ground."

20.

Puzzled, father said, "That's strange. We haven't had rain for days."

Wringles paused and explained, "Well, dad, you know how people leave the sprinklers on too long. By the way dad, now I know how we became such a great country and why we celebrate the Fourth of July."

His parents smiled with approval. Wringles talked about what he had learned about the birth of our country while having dinner with his family. His mother's cooking certainly tasted better than a can of beans.

21.

Westward Bound

Chapter Four

After Wringles finished his breakfast, he put on his red cap and rushed out the door to meet Sniggles who was anxiously waiting near the entrance. Wringles quickly climbed onto Sniggles' back and they were on their way to meet Kohana. Soon after they arrived at the tree where Kohana lived, they heard a loud, happy shriek and then Kohana glided down to greet his two happy friends. As soon as Wringles and Sniggles were secure on Kohana's back he flew high on a clear day and headed west.

Wringles asked, "Where are we going?"

"We're going to California." After flying for a few hours, Kohana landed under the shade of a tree. "While we're resting, I'll tell you more about the expansion of our country."

"Are you going to tell us about the War of 1812?" asked Sniggles.

"Thanks for reminding me. We went to war with Great Britain again because they were forcing American young men to serve in the British navy and army. Also, the British convinced the Indians to go to war against us while we were moving into Indian territory and another reason was to prove to the British that we also had a navy that was worthy of battle. The British always had the disadvantage of being so far from their homeland, making it difficult to replace fallen soldiers and supplies."

Wringles wondered, "What happened to the Indians after the war ended?"

"Before I answer that question, the American army made a serious blunder by burning down non-military buildings and looting the town of York in 1813; which was against the rules of war. The angry British wanted revenge. Consequently, they burned the White House, the U.S. Capital and other buildings in Washington D.C. on August 24, 1814, after they won the Battle of Bladensburg."

"What happened then?" asked Sniggles.

"The American Congress met elsewhere while the White House and Capital were being rebuilt. The British were satisfied that they had avenged the York incident and left to fight other battles. Soon after, victory was ours."

Kohana continued. "The Cherokee Indian nation was finally defeated and they were forced to give up their land east of the Mississippi. In 1838, President Andrew Jackson ordered 16,000 Cherokees to walk more than 2,000 miles to what is now the state of Oklahoma. Many Indians died on the long, arduous trail. The Cherokees called it "The Trail of Tears." It wasn't a proud moment in our history."

21.

Kohana added, "In order for our country to grow and prosper through trade it was essential to have a safe and a free access to the Mississippi River. President Jackson didn't want a foreign country as neighbors; so he decided it best to expand our country. He wanted to purchase western Tennessee and southwestern Kentucky; but the conservative "Whigs," wanted to limit our country to developing the existing land we already possessed."

"Looks like President Jackson had his way," said Sniggles.

" Yes, he did. Unfortunately, there were wars afterwards and many lives were lost. The addition of the Republic of Texas to our country in 1845 led to war with Mexico in 1846. I want to remind you that the slavery issue was not dead and it was revived when Texas became a state where slavery was still legal. Meantime, General Zachary Taylor defeated General Santa Anna's army in northern Mexico and General Scott led his army through Veracruz, captured Mexico City and won the war. The Treaty of Guadalupe Hidalgo was signed on February 2, 1848. Shortly before the treaty was signed, the Americans were badly defeated at the Alamo. Soon afterwards, Sam Houston, a Texas commander, led 700 men and defeated Santa Anna's army of 5,000 men. The American soldiers' and the peoples' battle cry was "Remember the Alamo.""

Wringles asked, "What was in the Treaty?"

"Well, the Rio Grande River became the southern boundary of Texas and a third of our country was added. The vast territories we acquired after the war ended became the states of California, Nevada, Utah, Colorado, Arizona and New Mexico. In addition, we paid 15,000,000 dollars to Mexico. The agreement in 1848, almost completed the United States."

"What happened after that?" asked Sniggles.

"Due to crowded conditions, the high cost of living, the promise of land ownership and the hope of great wealth, thousands of couageous people from the East and from other countries wanted to live in California."

Wringles asked, "How did people know how to get there?"

"Great question! Let me back up a little. President Jefferson wanted people to settle in the new territories; so, in 1804 he hired two men from Virginia, Merriwether Lewis and William Clark, to explore the vast Louisiana Purchase and to find safe passage to the Pacific Ocean. In their extensive journey they discovered new plants, animals, drew maps of rivers and found safe passage over mountain ranges. Also, our presence in the newly discovered land would prove to the Indians and to other countries that it was our land and we were determined to stay. Sacagawea, a brave fifteen year old Shoshone Indian 22.

who was a guide as well as an interpreter, helped Lewis and Clark whenever they met different Indian tribes. Her presence helped keep the peace with the different tribes."

Sniffles asked, "Then did more people go west?"

"Yes, they did, by the thousands. They went west by foot, horseback, stage coach and by wagon trains on the Oregon Trail. They had to cope with many hardships- such as Indian attacks, storms, the cold and the heat, small pox and shortages of food and water. In addition, they crossed rivers, pushed wagons through the mud and struggled over mountain passes. Years later, faster, more comfortable and safer ways to travel came about."

Wringles said, "You mean the invention of the steam engine and the building of railroads that carried people and things across the country?"

Sniggles added, "And the telegraph and the post office helped people communicate."

Surprised, Kohana nodded in agreement. "Also, the highways and trucks helped our country grow and prosper. Now, let's find out what also inspired thousands of people to go to California."

Kohana saved his energy by riding the columns of hot air that lifted him to great heights and then glided until he encountered another thermal. Wiggles and Sniffles enjoyed the panoramic view of deserts, mountain ranges, forests, farm land, herds cattle and sheep. However, when they flew into layers of smog over the cities, they all coughed and their eyes burned. They were relieved when Kohana changed course and they were soon flying above a series of white, fluffy clouds. Only the whispered sounds created by Kohana's wings flapping at a steady rhythm could be heard as he flew in sync with the aid of the friendly air currents. Finally, Kohana gently glided to a landing near an abandoned saw mill in the small town of Coloma, California.

Wringles remarked, "Why are we stopping here? What does this old, broken-down, wood building have to do with the growth of our country?"

Kohana smiled and asked, "Can either of you guess why pioneers risked their lives and endured hardships to go to California?"

Sniggles said, "I know. They heard about the warmer weather, land was free and it cost less."

Kohana said, That's true; but there's something else that appeals to everyone."

Wringles suddenly blurted out, "To get rich?"

23.

"Right! Gold was first discovered at this very spot, Sutter's saw mill, by James W. Marshall on January 24, 1848. He tried to keep it a secret; but that was impossible. Soon afterwards, over 250,000 people rushed to California by 1852. Half of them came by sea and the other half came by land on the California and the Gila River trails. President Polk officially declared a gold rush in 1849 and the gold prospectors were called the forty-niners.

"I bet many people got very rich," said Sniggles.

"That's not what happened. Only a very few struck it rich. Some of the men who weren't so lucky returned to their homes. A few of the men stayed and opened stores to sell supplies to gold prospectors. Others found ways to make a living. Also, many stayed because of the climate. Unfortunately, many boom towns went bust and became ghost towns when the gold ran out."

Wringles asked, "How did they look for gold?"

"Men panned for gold by using a tin pan to scoop up small amounts of gravel and sand from a creek bed and move the pan in a circular motion as the heavier gold flakes sunk to the bottom of the pan. Another way was to shovel gravel into a sluice box and the prospector would move a handle back and forth shaking the gold loose as water carried away the sand. Also, deep tunnels were dug in hill sides. The most damaging mining method was the use of powerful streams of water shot from large hoses, washing away hills and drastically changing and ruining the natural, beautiful landscape."

"Weren't there laws to prevent that?" asked Wringles

"Not in the beginning. Desperate gold prospectors stole land from the Indians and even killed hundreds of Indians all because of gold. It was a greedy, ruthless, lawless period in our history."

Sniggles commented, "I'm glad that those days are over."

Kohana added, "I should mention that President Lincoln in 1862, signed into law The Homestead Act. Each person received 160 acres of free federal land west of the Mississippi to farm or raise livestock. As years passed, other Homestead Acts followed to encourage more people to move west and to raise families."

Wringles said, "I guess that completes the story of how our country grew."

"Not quite. The country of Russia owned Alaska. It's a large piece of land that's much larger than Texas and only fur traders made a good living in a cold, desolate land. Russia was afraid that Great Britain would take their land if there were a war; so they

24.

decided to sell it. Great Britain didn't want it; but America did, thanks to the Secretary of State, William H. Seward, who had a difficult time convincing congress to buy "a frozen wilderness."

Sniggles asked, "How much did we pay for it?

"We paid 7,200,000 dollars for it in 1867 or about two cents an acre. William H. Seward was ridiculed by members of congress and by many Americans. The purchase of Alaska came to be known as "Seward's Folly.""

"Was it a mistake to buy Alaska?" asked Wringles

"Far from it. Gold was discovered and the result was the Great Klondike Gold Rush in 1896. In addition, oil, copper and diamonds were found in Alaska. It was an excellent investment and it eventually became a state. Today, most of Alaska is still in its natural state and it's the least populated state. In addition and more importantly, it proved to be a wise investment when we were at war with Japan during World War II. We were then able to defend and protect Alaska as well as defend our country."

"Now does that complete our country?" asked Sniggles.

"There's still more. James Gadsden, our ambassador to Mexico, arranged with Mexico to buy what is now southern Arizona and southwest New Mexico for 10,000,000 dollars. With the approval from congress, the purchase became official when Mexico's president and President Pierce signed the agreement in 1854. The Gadsden Purchase allowed a transcontinental railroad to pass through the southern states to promote trade and encourage people to settle in that part of the country."

Wringles asked, "Did the railroad companies buy land from the government?"

"No, the federal government wanted a faster and safer way for more people to travel to the vast, unsettled land west of the Mississippi; so it encouraged the railroad companies to build railroads by giving them free land and paying the companies generous amounts of money for each mile of track they laid. It was a great day of celebration when the Union Pacific Railroad from the East and the Central Pacific Railroad from the west finally met and connected their tracks at Promontory Summit, Utah, on May 10, 1869, to complete the first transcontinental railroad. Instead of months, it only took a few days to cross our vast country. Four gold ceremonial spikes were driven by prominent men from both companies and one is on display at Stanford University."

"Who built the railroads?" asked Wringles.

"Mostly the Irish and Chinese immigrants. Also, men from other countries helped install the large, wooden ties that supported the heavy twenty- foot sections of steel tracks, secured with steel spikes. They all worked hard and long hours in the freezing cold 25. and under the blazing sun for very low wages. They dug tunnels with only picks and shovels. Tracks were laid over mountains and on desert plains in all kinds of weather.

In order to enable trains to. run in the winter, snow sheds were built over the tracks in the mountains. Also, telegraph poles were installed alongside the tracks to support telegraph wires that carried messages for many miles."

Sniggles said, "I bet that the Indians didn't like trains going through their land."

"You're exactly right. It became a serious and a dangerous situation. The Indians often attacked the trains pulled by the "Iron Horses." Railroad companies had to hire men with guns to protect the railroads and passengers."

Kohana looked at Sniggles and asked, "What have you learned so far?"

Smiling with confidence, "A lot was really happening at that time. The Civil war was going on and President Lincoln was assassinated. Also, we bought land from different countries, had a gold rush, built railroads and thousands of people moved west."

"I guess it's much better to buy the land than to go to war," Wringles concluded.

"That's correct. The last two states to be officially added to our country were Alaska and Hawaii in 1959," said Kohana.

Wringles proudly stated, "Now I know why we have fifty stars in our flag."

Sniggles remarked, "Our great country's growth was really interesting."

Kohana said, "Yes it was and I only told you part of our history. Courageous pioneers often faced constant danger and worked hard. They sacrificed a great deal and many people lost their lives in wars and in settling the West so you and I can live comfortably in a safe country."

Suddenly, the earth started to shake. Wringles and Sniggles became frightened. "What's going on?" asked Sniffles.

"Don't worry. California is known to have earthquakes."

"What shall we do? Look! The ground is starting to split!" panicked Wringles

"We're done here. Hop on. We'll be safe in the air."

Kohana took a detour to show Sniggles and Wringles the vast blue Pacific Ocean. They became quite excited when they saw hump-back whales migrating south and the large container ships carrying cargo to and from other countries. 26.

Also, the large, luxurious cruise ships were quite impressive. Sniggles and Wringles were thrilled to see the world famous Golden Gate Bridge. The panoramic view of the sail boats in the San Francisco Bay cutting through the waves as the strong winds filled their sails was spectacular. Adding to the beautiful seascape and California's long coast with its many popular beaches, were sea gulls flying about and seals basking in the sun.

On their way back home, Kohana decided to fly northeast to show his friends Mt. Rushmore in the Black Hills of South Dakota. As soon as Kohana landed on George Washington's head, Wringles asked.

"Why are we stopping on this mountain?"

Kohana answered, "I thought that it was important for both of you to see this special place since it's a famous historical landmark. If you look around, you'll see the heads of four famous presidents carved in granite."

Sniggles exclaimed, "Wow they're big! Who carved these heads?"

"A Danish American, Gutzon Borglum and his son. The sculptures are sixty foot tall."

"Who are they?"

They are George Washington, Thomas Jefferson, Theodore Roosevelt and Abraham Lincoln."

Sniggles asked, "Why were these four presidents chosen?"

"They were selected because they had contributed so much to our country's beginning, the preservation of basic principles in the constitution and our country's expansion. The sculptures were started in 1927 and they were not completed until 1941."

Both Wringles and Sniggles were overwhelmed and speechless by the size and the years it took.

Kohana said, " I knew that you would be impressed. Take one last look. It's time to go."

Curious, Wringles asked, "Before we leave, Would you tell us about President Roosevelt?

"Yes. I'm glad that you asked. Roosevelt overcame a sick childhood with healthy foods and plenty of exercise. He had a strong interest in nature and he studied biology at a very young age. He learned so much about nature that Roosevelt was considered to be a Naturalist. He was a hero in the Spanish-American War as a member of the Rough Riders where he demonstrated great courage, leadership and skill. He decided to enter politics and he eventually became vice president under President Mckinley.

27.

When President Mckinley was assassinated, Roosevelt became the president.

One of the first laws he signed into law was the Pure Food and Drug Act to help protect the health of all people. Another important accomplishment was to break up large corporations and railroads with new regulations in order to control their size and to limit their powers."

"He really did a lot!" exclaimed Sniggles.

"Yes, he did and there's more. He created five national parks, preserved vast areas of forests, saved several national monuments and continued to protect and preserve our natural resources. The impossible task of building the Panama Canal in Central America under the harshest of conditions was one of his greatest achievements as president. Hundreds of workers had become ill and died because of yellow fever and malaria until a scientist, William C. Gorges, discovered that mosquitoes were the cause. By eliminating standing water and spraying mosquito breeding grounds, the problem was resolved and the canal was completed without loss of life.

President Roosevelt also expanded our navy. He arranged to have our "White Fleet" tour the world to show other countries that we were a naval power. Roosvelt believed in "Speaking softly and carrying a big stick." Also, he was awarded the Nobel Peace Prize for helping end the Russo-Japanese War. Now you can understand why he's a member of this group of great presidents."

Wringles and Sniggles smiled and nodded in agreement. Satisfied, they climbed onto Kohana's back and off he flew among the fleecy, white clouds scattered in a background of a blue sky.

The long flight home was trouble free. Tired, Wringles and Sniggles slept most of the way. After landing near Kohana's tree, the three close friends made plans for future trips to learn about the unique qualities of each state and to visit our beautiful national parks. As soon as Wringles returned home, the family all wiggled with joy. After dinner, the family sat in a circle and Wringles shared what he and his friend, Sniggles, had been taught by Kohana, a brave and a wise friend.

28.

Printed in the United States
by Baker & Taylor Publisher Services